This Little Tiger book belongs to:

_____

_____

_____

For Noah x

LITTLE TIGER PRESS
1 The Coda Centre, 189 Munster Road,
London SW6 6AW
www.littletiger.co.uk
First published in Great Britain 2001
by Little Tiger Press, London
This edition published 2012
Text and illustrations
copyright © Tim Warnes 2001
Visit Tim Warnes at
www.ChapmanandWarnes.com
Tim Warnes has asserted his right
to be identified as the author
and illustrator of this work under the
Copyright, Designs and Patents Act, 1988

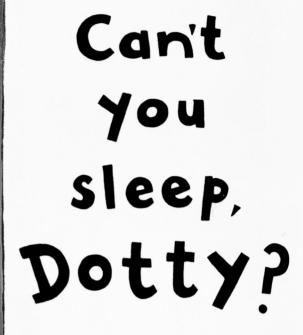

Can't you sleep, Dotty?

★ ★ ★

Tim Warnes

LITTLE TIGER PRESS

Dotty couldn't sleep.
It was her first night
in her new home.

She tried sleeping
upside down.

She tried
snuggling up
with Penguin.

She even tried
lying on the
floor.

AWOOOOOOOOOOOoo

But still Dotty
couldn't sleep.

Dotty's howling woke up Pip the
mouse. "Can't you sleep, Dotty?"
he asked. "Perhaps you should try
counting the stars like I do."

But Dotty could only count up to one. *That* wasn't enough to send her to sleep.

What could she do next?

AWOOOOOOOOOO

Susie the bird was awake now. "Can't you sleep, Dotty?" she twittered. "I always have a little drink before I go to bed."

Dotty went to her bowl
and took a drink.

But then she made
a little puddle.
Well *that*
didn't help!
What *could* Dotty
do to get to sleep?

AWOOOOOOOOOo

Whiskers the rabbit had woken up, too.
"Can't you sleep, Dotty?" he mumbled
sleepily. "I hide away in my burrow
at bedtime. That always works."

Dotty dived under her blanket so that
only her bottom was showing. But it was
all dark under there with no light at all.

Dotty was too scared to go to sleep.

AWOOOOOOOOOOooo

Tommy the tortoise
poked his head from
out of his shell.

"Can't you sleep, Dotty?" he sighed. "I like
to sleep where it's bright and sunny."

Dotty liked that idea . . .

. . . and turned on her flashlight!

"Turn it off, Dotty!"
shouted all her friends.
"*We* can't get to sleep now!"

Poor Dotty was too
tired to try anything else.
Then Tommy had a great idea . . .

He helped Dotty into her bed.
What Dotty needed for the first
night in her new home was . . .

. . . to snuggle up among *all* her new friends. Soon they were all fast asleep.

Night night, Dotty!